"A capful, do you call it?" said I. "It was a terrible storm."

"A storm, you fool," he replied, "why, that was nothing at all. If you plan to sail, you'll need to get used to much worse than that."

The worse came sooner than anyone expected. Eight days into our journey, the wind increased again. It blew a terrible storm indeed. I began to see terror and amazement even in the faces of the seasoned sailors. I thought the danger had passed, but when the master himself said that we should all be lost, I was dreadfully frightened. The sea went mountains high and broke over us every three or four minutes. But the worse was yet to come.

We had sprung a leak. One man said four feet of water filled the hold. All hands were called to the pump.

We worked on, but the water increased in the hold. The ship was sinking. The storm began to clear, but we could not make it to a port. The master fired his guns for help, and a light ship, out ahead of us, sent a small boat to save us. The men on the boat risked their lives rescuing us, but they managed to get us safely aboard. As we rowed toward shore, we saw our ship sink.

After much labored rowing, we reached the shore and were safe. Two or three days later, I met with my friend, who had asked me to join him on this trip. He told his father, who was master of the ship, who I was, and that I had joined them just to learn about sailing. His father said to me with a very grave and concerned tone, "Young man, you ought never to go to sea anymore. You ought to take this for a plain and visible token that you are not to be a seafaring man."

We parted soon after. I didn't know what to do, so I headed back to my home and family. Then it occurred to me how my neighbors would laugh at me, and my parents would be ashamed of my foolishness. No. I decided to sail once again and try to seek my fortune on the sea.

—◠—

I boarded a vessel bound for the coast of Africa. The master of the ship was a good man who liked me. I was to be his messmate and companion. This adventure was a success. Though I was seasick much of time, I learned to be a sailor. I also made some money through trading.

I was now set up to be a trader. To my great sadness, my friend, the ship's master, died shortly after our return. I decided to go on the same journey again with his mate from the former voyage. This was the unhappiest voyage that ever man made.

As our ship made its way toward the Canary Islands, a Turkish pirate ship surprised us. A chase began. For hours we tried to outrun the pirates. We prepared to fight, our ship having twelve guns. The pirates had eighteen. We exchanged shots, but it did no good. Sixty pirates climbed upon our decks. They began cutting and hacking the decks and rigging. Our ship was disabled. Three of our men were killed and eight were wounded. We surrendered and were taken as prisoners to Sallee, a port belonging to the Moors.

Because I was young and nimble, I was made the captain's slave. When he went to sea, he left me on shore to look after his little garden and to do housework. When he came home again from his cruise, he ordered me to look after the ship.

For two years, I imagined my escape, but I had no way of putting it into practice. Then, I saw my chance. My master frequently took me and another slave out on a fishing boat. I was a good fisherman and he never went without me. One time a fog quickly settled in, and we lost sight of the shore. Then a wind blew up and we were almost lost. It took hours to find our way back.

Warned by this disaster, my master decided to take better care of himself.

He ordered a larger, sturdier boat that could ride out a storm. He would keep food and water on it, along with powder and shot. He would use the vessel for hunting birds as well as fishing.

One day, he planned to take some important men out on the boat. He asked me to load it up with extra food, water, and gunpowder. While my master left me to do this, I had an idea. I would load the boat not for his pleasure, but for my escape.

I was helped in my plan by two fellow slaves, Moely, and a young boy called Xury. They did not know what I was up to. They merely followed my orders to load the boat according to our master. Once the boat was loaded, I suggested that we catch some fish for our master's enjoyment. We sailed out.

Secretly, whenever I caught a fish, I would let it go. I said, "This will not do. There are no fish here. We must sail further out."

We had gone quite a distance. I stepped toward Moely and, making as if I stooped for something behind him, I tossed him overboard. He was very much surprised and begged me to take him along. I told him to swim for the shore, or I would kill him. He headed for the shore. I have no doubt that he reached it with ease, for he was an excellent swimmer.

Then I turned to the boy and said, "Xury, if you will be faithful to me I'll make you a great man; but if you will not, I'll throw you into the sea, too."

The boy smiled in my face and spoke so innocently that I could not mistrust him. He swore to be faithful to me, and go all over the world with me.

We sailed for five days. I was certain that by now the Moors had stopped looking for us. We arrived at a coast, but I knew not where we were—what nation, what country. I saw no people. All I wanted was fresh water. In the evening, we anchored our ship in sight of a creek. We thought we would swim ashore as soon as it was dark. But once the sun went down and darkness fell, we heard dreadful noises of the barking, roaring, and howling of wild creatures. We didn't know what kinds of animals made these sounds. The poor boy was ready to die with fear and begged me not to go ashore until daylight.

We stayed in the boat, but slept little. We saw vast great creatures (we knew not what to call them) of many sorts come down to the seashore and run into the water, wallowing and washing themselves for the pleasure of cooling themselves. They made such hideous howlings and yellings, of which I never heard the like.

Xury was dreadfully frightened, and so was I. But we were both more frightened when we heard one of these mighty creatures come swimming towards our boat. We could not see him, but knew him to be a monstrous and furious beast by his blowing. Xury said it was a lion, and it might have been for all I knew. Poor Xury cried to me to weigh anchor and row away. I said no.

Then I saw the creature (whatever it was) within two oars' length, which surprised me. I immediately stepped to the cabin door, and taking up my gun, fired it. He immediately turned about and swam towards the shore again.

In the morning, we needed to go ashore for water, for we had not a pint left. We approached the land carefully, fearing not just wild animals, but savages. Happily, we met neither. We filled our jars with fresh water and Xury shot a rabbit for us to eat. Then we sailed some more.

We moved southward for ten or twelve days, eating and drinking very little. We were following what I believed to be the coast of Africa. I hoped to spy a European ship. It was our only hope of survival.

Ten days later, we saw people standing along the shore, watching us. They were stark naked. Only one carried a weapon, which was a sharp stick. I wanted to go ashore, but Xury was afraid. He said the stick was a lance, which can be thrown a great way with good aim. We kept our distance, but talked with them by signs as well as I could. I tried to tell them I needed something to eat. They beckoned me to stop the boat so they could fetch meat.

I lowered the sail and two of them ran off, only to return with dried meat and some corn. We were willing to accept it, but didn't know what to do next. I was not going to come ashore to them, and they were as much afraid of us. Then they thought to lay the food on the shore and back away, so that we could come and pick it up.

We made signs of thanks to them. Then from out of the mountains suddenly came two mighty creatures, one chasing the other. Whether they were in sport or in rage, we could not tell. The people on the shore scattered in fear. Then the creatures ran into the ocean and swam about. They were heading straight for our boat. I quickly loaded my gun and fired, killing one. The other, fearful of the noise and fire, fled back into the mountains. The people also were frightened. They had never seen or heard a gun before, and some of them fainted at the sound of it.

They were happy we killed the beast. They pulled it to the shore with ropes and cut it up to eat. Now that we were friends, they gave us more food and water for our journey. We thanked them and sailed on.

—w—

At long last, we spied a ship in the distance. We waved our flags of distress and fired a gun to attract attention. The ship sailed to our rescue and the captain bade us to come aboard.

To express my joy over being saved from our miserable condition, I offered the captain everything I had. He told me he wanted nothing from me, but that I be delivered safely to Brazil. From there I could make my way back home.

When we arrived in Brazil, the captain gave me a fair price for my boat. He also offered me sixty pieces of eight for the boy, Xury. I didn't want to sell the boy's freedom, for he had helped me to become free. The captain assured me that he would set Xury free after ten years, and Xury himself was willing to stay with the captain, so I let him go.

I went to work on a plantation in Brazil, and was soon able to buy land of my own. Over the years, my plantation did very well. In four years I thrived and prospered, but still I wanted adventure.

It happened that I was talking with some merchants and planters who were preparing to send a ship to Africa. They asked me to join the ship so I could manage their affairs once it arrived there. I agreed to the voyage. I put my plantation in order and went on board the first of September, 1659. It was the same day I had left my family so many years before.

The ship carried six guns and fourteen men, besides the master, his boy, and myself. We had good weather, only very hot, as we followed Brazil's coast. About twelve days out, when no land was in sight, a violent hurricane surprised us. For another twelve days we could do nothing but let it carry us wherever fate and the fury of the winds directed. Each day I expected to be swallowed up. None of us expected to survive.

In this distress, besides the terror of the storm, one of our men died of fever, and one man and the boy washed overboard.

The weather began to grow a little calmer, but the ship was leaky and very much disabled. We hoped to reach one of our English islands when a second storm came upon us. It drove us far from where ships usually sail. Now, even if our ship survived and we made land, we were in danger of being devoured by savages rather than returning to our own country.

Early one morning, while the wind was still blowing very hard, one of our men cried out, "Land!" and no sooner than we ran out of our cabin to look, than the ship struck upon sand. The sea broke over the ship so strongly that we thought we should perish right then.

We didn't know where we were. We didn't know if the land before us was an island or the mainland. We expected death at any moment. The ship seemed like it would break into pieces. To escape, the eleven of us headed into a boat. The sea was wild and high, but we had no choice. As the wind drove us nearer and nearer the shore, the land looked more frightful than the sea.

Suddenly a raging wave, like a mountain, crashed over us, upsetting the boat and separating us. We were all swallowed up in a moment. Though I swam very well, I could not escape from the waves to catch my breath. The water carried me a good way toward the shore and left me on almost dry land. But I was half-dead with the water I took in. I got upon my feet and went onto the shore before another wave could sweep me away. But that was impossible. The sea came after me as high as a great hill, and as furious as an enemy. I had no strength to fight it. I held my breath and tried to float.

The wave buried me in water twenty or thirty feet deep. I held my breath tight until I felt I would burst. The water carried me with great force onto the shore. I felt myself rising up until my hands and head shot above the surface. I gasped for air.

I was now landed, and safe on shore. I walked about, thinking of my situation. I looked at the stranded ship. It lay so far off I could hardly see it. I wondered how I ever made it to shore. No one else had survived. I was grateful for being saved from the sea, but my joy soon left me. I was wet, I had no clothes, nor anything to eat or drink. I could see that my fate was to die of hunger, or to be devoured by wild beasts. I had no weapons with which to defend myself or hunt for food.

Night was coming. I ran about like a madman, thinking about the wild animals on the island. I walked along the shore and, to my great joy, found fresh water to drink. Then I climbed into a tree so that I might sleep away from any wild animals that might want to eat me. I was so tired that I slept deeply.

When I awoke, it was broad day. The ship had been driven within a mile of the shore where I was. I hoped to get to it so I could find something to eat or drink or wear.

By noon, the tide went out, and I could come within a quarter of a mile of the ship. I pulled off my clothes, for the weather was hot, and swam to the wrecked ship. I found a rope to pull myself aboard. The hold was full of water, but I found that all the ship's provisions were dry. Being hungry, I went to the breadroom and filled my pockets with biscuits, and ate as I went. Now I wanted nothing but a boat, so I could take supplies back to dry land.

It was foolish to sit still and wish for what I didn't have. I picked up boards and spare masts. I tied them with rope so they wouldn't float away, and then tossed them overboard. When this was done, I went down the ship's side and tied four of them together, forming a raft. Then I lay two or three short pieces across them, but it couldn't bear much weight. I found a carpenter's saw to cut a spare topmast into three lengths and added them to my raft. It was now strong enough to carry supplies.

I carefully loaded it with bread, rice, three Dutch cheeses, five pieces of dried goat's flesh, and a small bit of grain. There had been some barley and wheat, but to my disappointment, the rats had eaten or spoiled it all.

While I was loading the raft, I noticed the tide began to flow. The clothes I left on the shore swam out to sea. I was left only with the open-kneed britches I was wearing. Searching the ship, I found more than enough clothes, but took only what I needed for right now. It was more important for me to collect tools. I found the carpenter's chest, which for me was more valuable than gold.

These things I loaded onto my raft, along with ammunition, guns, powder, and swords. Then I set back to the land. I had three things in my favor: One, a smooth, calm sea. Two, the tide rising and setting in to the shore. Three, what little wind there was, blew me towards the land. I found two broken oars on the ship, which helped me, too. For a mile or thereabouts my raft went very well.

The raft drifted with the current caused by a creek running off the land. I spied a little cove on the right shore of the creek. With great pain and difficulty, I guided my raft there. I fastened her by sticking my two broken oars into the ground where it was safe.

—m—

My next job was to view the country and seek a proper place to live. I took one of my weapons and climbed a steep hill. There I discovered that I was on an island. No land was to be seen except some rocks that lay a great way off, and two small islands closer than this, but still far off. Nothing seemed to live on this island, except perhaps for wild beasts. I saw a wide variety of birds. I had never seen any like them before. I could not tell what was fit for food and what was not. As I came down from the hill, I shot at a great bird sitting upon a tree at the edge of a great wood. I believe it was the first gun that had been fired there since

For a mile or thereabouts my raft went very well.

the creation of the world. I had no sooner fired but from all parts of the wood came all sorts of birds, making confused screaming, crying sounds.

The creature I killed looked like a hawk. I found its flesh wasn't good to eat.

I went back to my raft and began to unload my cargo. It took me the rest of the day. By nighttime, I wasn't sure where to sleep. I was afraid to lie down on the ground, not knowing if some wild beast would devour me. I took the chests and boards I had brought on shore and made a little hut. I didn't know what I was going to do for food.

Over the next several days, I made more trips to the wrecked ship. I carried back all that I could. I had built myself a little tent to sleep in. After thirteen days on shore, I made eleven trips to the ship. I had taken almost everything out of it. On my twelfth trip, the wind began to rise. Working quickly, I found some knives and razors. I also found pieces of eight and gold and silver. "What good is money here?" I said to myself. "The knives are worth more than any amount of coin." But I took the money anyway.

The sea was now too rough to sail my raft back to shore, so I had to swim. It was difficult carrying my treasures with me, but after much labor, I made it safely to shore. I climbed into my tent and went to sleep as the winds blew all around me that night. In the morning, when I looked out, I was surprised to see that the ship was gone. The wind had destroyed it.

Now I had to think about keeping safe from savages or wild beasts. I had not seen any, but I needed to be careful.

I found a shallow cave on the side of a steep hill. I pitched a tent in front of it. It provided shelter from the sun and a view of the sea, in case I should see a ship sail nearby.

In a wide area around the tent, I built a fence of sharpened stakes. This fence was so strong that neither man nor beast could get into it, or over it. It took a great deal of time and labor to cut the stakes and drive them into the earth.

I had no door to get into my home. Instead, I built a ladder to go over the top of the fence. After I climbed in, I pulled the ladder behind me. Nothing could follow me inside this fortress.

Safely inside, I built a bigger tent from the ship's sails. I also dug a cave in the ground behind it, which was a sort of cellar. Everything I saved from the ship was safe within.

Then one night, a storm blew in. A sudden flash of lightning and great clap of thunder struck fear into me. O my gunpowder! My very heart sunk within me when I thought that with one blast, all my powder might be destroyed. I needed the powder to fire my guns so that I could hunt for food or fight against enemies. My life depended on that powder, and I realized it could be gone in an instant. I wasn't worried about my own safety if the powder should explode. If that happened, I would never have known what hit me.

After the storm, I separated the powder into smaller bags. Then I stored these bags in different places, so they would be safe.

I found wild goats living on the island. They were shy and fast, and it was difficult to hunt them. But then I taught myself how to do it. If they were eating in the valley, I would head for high ground, where they took no notice of me. Then I would be able to shoot them for their meat. I made my cave bigger, so I could build a fire and cook in it.

I believed that my life would end on this terrible island. The tears ran down my face when I thought about it. I felt like the most unlucky person on earth. Then I thought about the other ten men on the ship who lost their lives in the storm. I realized that perhaps I was not so bad off.

It occurred to me that I should keep a record of how many days I had been on the island. I cut a large wooden post and making it into a great cross, I set it up on the shore where I first landed. With my knife, I cut into it the words: "I came on shore here on the 30th of September, 1659." On the sides of this square post I cut one notch for every day I was here.

We had on the ship a dog and two cats. I had carried the cats to the island. The dog had jumped out of the ship himself and swam on shore with me. He was a trusty servant to me for many years. He would keep me company and fetch things.

—⁓—

What I really wanted were tools. I had a pen, but not much ink. I needed a spade, a pick-axe, and a shovel. Without them, my work was difficult. Even simple tasks took days to finish. I was in misery. To cheer myself up, I made a list of what was good and what was evil with my situation:

Evil	Good
I am cast upon a horrible island, with no chance of being found.	*I am alive, and not drowned as the rest of my ship's company was.*
I am separated from the rest of the world to be miserable.	*I have been singled out to be spared from death, and miraculously saved.*
I am separated from human society.	*I am not starved.*
I have no clothes to cover me.	*I am in a hot climate, and if I had clothes, I could scarcely wear them.*

I set it up on the shore where I first landed.

Evil	Good
I am without any defense or means to resist any violence of man or beast.	*I am cast on an island where I see no wild beasts to hurt me. I could have been ship-wrecked on more dangerous shores.*
I have no soul to speak to.	*The ship was near enough to the shore so I could collect so many necessary things to survive here.*

Studying the list, I realized the good outweighed the evil, and that lifted my spirits. A year and a half passed. I added to my home and covered it with a thatched roof to keep out the rain. I taught myself how to build a table and chair so I could be comfortable. I put up shelves. During the rainy season, I stayed indoors except to hunt for food.

While hunting, I killed one goat and wounded another in the leg. I led the injured goat home on a string. Then I splinted and bandaged the broken leg. I took good care of the little goat, and it grew strong as ever. From my nursing it, it grew tame. It ate the green plants in my yard and would not go away. This was the first time I thought of taming some creatures so that I might have food when my gunpowder and shot was gone.

Sorting through my belongings, I found the pouch of spoiled grain that the rats had gotten into on the ship. The grain was useless, so I dumped it onto the ground in order to use the pouch for something else. I didn't think about it again until several weeks later. I was surprised to see that the grain was growing— eight or twelve ears of barley came up, along with some rice. I was excited and I wondered if I could one day find a way to make bread.

I spent three or four months of hard labor building a second wall around my home. I wanted the wall to hide my home, blending it into the forest. I had just about finished it when I was almost killed in a terrifying way. All of a sudden the ceiling of my cave began to throw dirt down. And from the edge of the hill over my head, the two posts I set up cracked frightfully. I thought my cave would collapse, so I ran out. But it wasn't just the cave. The wall and my ladder shook, too. I realized that I was in an earthquake. The ground I stood on shook three times. Each was mighty enough to bring down the strongest building. I had never felt anything like it. I didn't know what to do. I was afraid to go back into my home for fear it would fall and crush me.

That was not the end of my troubles. As I sat outside, I saw the sky grow cloudy with rain. The sea grew black and covered with froth and foam. A hurricane blew, tearing trees up by the roots and whipping the island with wind. It went on for three hours before settling down. Then it was calm, and it began to rain very hard.

All this while I sat upon the ground, very terrified and alone. Soon I realized that the hurricane was caused by the earthquake. Now that it was over, I could go back into my cave again. I did not sleep well, for fear of the cave falling on me.

The next day, I decided to build another place to live. This new place would not be at the bottom of a hill, so that big rocks couldn't tumble upon me. But until I could build my new home, I needed to fix up the old one so I could live here safely.

Before I could get started, I grew ill. I shivered as if the weather had been cold. I could not rest for the violent pains in my head. I sweated and shivered and felt feverish for seven days. I had very little to eat, and was too weak to hunt. Never was I more miserable. Slowly I began to get better. I walked about, but was very weak. At night I made my supper of three turtle's eggs, which I roasted in the ashes and ate in the shell.

After I had eaten, I tried to walk, but was so weak that I could hardly carry a gun (which I never went without). I sat, watching the sea, and rested. The next few days went on like this, until my recovery was nearly complete. When I felt better, I thanked God aloud for my recovery. In the morning I took out the Bible; and beginning at the New Testament, I began seriously to read it. I found encouragement in the words I read.

I accepted the fact that I would spend the rest of my life on the island. I began to explore my new land more completely. My survey began at the creek where I left my raft. I followed it to a pleasant meadow covered with grass. Around it were many large plants that I had never seen before. I searched for familiar ones that I knew were good to eat, but I found none.

The next day, I explored beyond the meadow. The country became more woody. I found melons growing on the ground and many grapes in the trees. The vines had spread everywhere and the grapes were very ripe and rich. This was a surprising discovery, and I was glad. I picked many of them and left them to dry in the sun to become raisins.

Night fell, and I spent it in the woods. It was the first time I didn't return to my home to sleep. To be safe from any wild animals, I climbed a tree and slept in its branches.

The next day, I walked further on. I came over a hill to a spring of fresh water with lovely plants growing all around. It looked like a garden, and it made me happy to think that this beauty was all my own. This was my personal country.

I found cocoa trees, orange, and lemon, and citron trees. But all were wild and very few had fruit. Some limes were ripe. I gathered them and mixed their juice with water. It was very cool and refreshing. I gathered some of these fruits to bring

All this while I sat upon the ground, very terrified and alone.

back to my cave. They would be good to have for the rainy season, which I knew was approaching. But I so liked this place that I built a second home here. I called it my country house. My original cave I called my seacoast house.

By the time the rains came in August, I had stored away much food, including two hundred bunches of raisins. From mid-August through mid-October it rained every day. Sometimes it came down so hard that I could not leave my cave for several days. On less rainy days, I hunted and killed a goat and a tortoise. The tortoise's eggs provided me with many meals.

After the rainy season, the grain that I planted had grown. I harvested the seeds and prepared a field to sow them. I didn't sow all the seeds at once, and that was a good thing. I planted the first batch during the dry season, and they failed to come up. I was more careful with the second batch. By experimenting, I learned exactly when the proper season was to sow. I could plant and harvest two times each year.

The grain was not all that was growing. I was surprised to learn that the fence posts I had cut to surround my country house had also taken root. To my pleasure, they became young trees. I pruned them and allowed them to grow into a sturdy, living wall. Their branches provided shade.

Carrying anything was difficult because I had no large vessels. I taught myself how to weave baskets to carry my grapes and fruit in. But I had nothing except small jars to carry water, and no pot to cook in. I spent many months trying to make pots of clay. They were ugly, lumpy and weak. I didn't give up, and after many tries, I was successful. Now I had jugs to carry water and pots to boil meat for stew.

—◊◊◊—

In the morning I took out the Bible.

I continued to explore the island, and traveled to the far side of it. The day was bright and clear when I arrived on the opposite shore. In the distance, I could see land about forty miles away. I didn't know what part of the world I was in, so I could not guess what land that might be. It could be an island or a continent. I wondered if savages or cannibals lived there. Once again, I was thankful for being shipwrecked in a safe place.

As I walked, I saw many parrots. I managed to catch a young one. I hoped to tame it and teach it to talk, so that I might have a companion besides the dog and cats. This side of the island had several kinds of animals. Many were good to hunt and eat. In this journey, my dog surprised a young kid and injured it. I saved the little goat from the dog and brought it home with me. I built a small pen for it, and a cage for my parrot, Poll. In time, both Poll and the goat became quite tame.

When I was kept indoors because of the rain, I would talk to Poll and teach him to speak. I quickly taught him to know his own name, and at last to speak it out pretty loud. "Poll" was the first word I ever heard spoken on the island by any mouth but my own.

I had been on the island two years, and I began to feel happy and comfortable with my life here. I captured and tamed more goats. They provided me with ample meat without having to hunt. I was able to save my limited supply of powder and shot. The goats also provided me with milk and cheese.

My crops grew, as well, but with difficulty. I was happy to see the grain coming up, but I was in danger of losing it to all sorts of enemies. The goats and wild hares lay in it night and day. They bit off the tender leaves as they came up.

All I could do was fence the crop in with a hedge. It took a great deal of work, and it had to be done quickly to save the plants. Until it was done, I would shoot the intruders during the day, and have my dog stand guard all night. As soon as the grain ripened, it faced a new threat. The birds came to eat the seeds. Scarecrows frightened them off, and my crops grew in peace.

At the end of December, the grain was ready. I reaped it in my way, for I cut off nothing but the ears, and carried it away in a great basket, which I had made. I had nearly two bushels of rice and more than two and a half bushels of barley. When the season came around again, I planted much of this new seed. When I harvested it, I had about twenty bushels of barley and at least that much rice. I decided to plant a crop of this every year, and bake the rest into bread. But how to do it?

To grind the grain, I found a big block of hard wood. With an axe and hatchet, I carved a hollow space in the center. I carved another piece of hard wood into a heavy beater. Next I put some grain in the hollowed-out wood and crushed it into flour with the beater. I found some old cloth to use as a sieve, so I could separate the useful grain from the chaff. It took days of labor, but at last I had flour.

To bake my bread, I built an oven out of clay. I would cover it with glowing embers. The heat would cook my loaves. I had no yeast, so these loaves were flat, but satisfying.

I began to think about life on the land that I could see from my island. What if the people living there were not savages or cannibals? Was there any way I could possibly get there? I began to build a canoe.

I went into the forest to find a large tree that I could carve into a canoe. It had to be big enough to carry me and my food and supplies. Once I found the tree, it took twenty days to cut it down, because my tools were not good. I spent fourteen more days cutting the branches and limbs off. Then, four months to

shape it and carve out the inside with a mallet and a chisel. While I was working on it, I passed my fourth year on the island. I hoped it would be my last. Finally, the canoe was complete. I was delighted. All I had to do was get it into the water—but I found that it was too big for me to move! The canoe was very heavy, and to get to the sea, I had to drag it uphill. I could not even budge it. Nothing I did could make it move. I had to leave it in the woods, to my great sadness.

Another year went by. I built another canoe, a smaller one. It was as big as I could manage, but too small to sail forty miles to the other land. Instead, I thought I would try to sail it close to my island. I fitted up a little mast to my boat, and made a sail out of a piece of the ship's sail. I found that the little boat sailed very well; and thus I every now and then took a little voyage upon the sea. I never went far.

In my sixth year, I decided take the boat around the entire island and explore. I would stop here and there, tie the boat up, and inspect the land. On my third day, the sea was calm, but a swift current lay beneath the surface. It carried my boat along with such violence that I could not get back to shore. Paddling did nothing. I thought I would be lost at sea and starve to death. However, I worked hard and was able to break free of the current. With much labor I paddled back to my island, near exhaustion.

I tucked the boat into the woods and crossed the island to get back to my home. I got over the fence and laid down in the shade to rest, and soon fell asleep. I dreamed that someone was calling me: "Robin, Robin, Robin Crusoe, poor Robin Crusoe! Where are you? Where have you been?"

I was so dead asleep at first that I didn't awaken fully. But as the voice continued to repeat "Robin Crusoe, Robin Crusoe," at last I began to wake up.

I reaped it in my way, for I cut off nothing but the ears . . .

The voice was real, and continued to call. At first I was dreadfully frightened. But no sooner were my eyes open than I saw my Poll sitting on the top of the hedge. My parrot had learned the words so perfectly.

—∞—

In time, I built another small boat to use on the side of the island I lived on. I never went far with it and was very cautious. It happened one day, about noon, I was going toward my boat when I had another great surprise. It was the print of a man's naked foot on the shore, pressed into the sand. I stood like one thunderstruck, or as if I had seen an apparition. I listened, I looked round me, I could hear nothing, nor see anything. I went up a hill to look further. I went up the shore and down the shore. I could find no other footprint but that one.

How it got there, I had no idea. It left me confused and terrified. I went back to my hidden home. On the way I looked behind me at every two or three steps, mistaking every bush and tree, every stump for a man. I fled into my castle (for that is what I called my house) like I was being pursued. That night, I could not sleep.

I was glad that the person who left the print did not see me. I wondered if he could have been a savage from the mainland who was driven by currents to my island. Maybe he won't come back. Or maybe more will come back, and they would destroy my crops, my livestock, and my home. Perhaps they will come back to eat me. For three days I did not leave my castle, so afraid was I. Then I thought that perhaps my mind was playing tricks on me. Maybe the footprint was my own.

Still frightened, I went back to the place where I saw the footprint. I was ready

Thus I every now and then took a little voyage upon the sea.

to run for my life at any moment. When I got to the print, it was still there. I measured it against my own foot. The strange print was bigger than my foot. Someone else had been here to make it. For fifteen years, I had seen no one on the island. Now somebody else had found it.

I reinforced my castle in case the stranger returned. I built the walls thicker and put in slots to fire my muskets through. I planted a wall of stakes that began to grow. In two years' time I had a thick grove. In five or six years I had a wood before my dwelling. It was so monstrous thick and strong that no one could get past it. No one would guess that a home stood behind it.

To keep my herd of goats safe, I thought it best to separate them into two groups. That way, if the strangers came back and found one group, the other would be safe. I went to great pains finding a good place and building a fence. Every night I expected to be murdered and devoured by morning. This was all because of a single footprint in the sand. Soon I had more reason to fear.

While inspecting another part of the island one day, I came down a hill to the shore. It is not possible for me to express the horror of my mind at seeing the shore spread with skulls, hands, feet, and other bones of human bodies. There also were the remains of a fire pit, where the savages sat down to cook and eat their fellow humans.

I went back to my part of the island and stayed there for two years. I never strayed far from my home in the woods. I was cautious about firing my gun, for fear they would hear it. I hunted by traps and snares instead. I stopped building things because of the noise I made, and I lit as few fires as possible, to avoid the rising smoke.

—⚹—

I stood like one thunderstruck, or as if I had seen an apparition.

One night, in my twenty-third year on the island, I was out before sunrise to harvest my grain. I was surprised to see a campfire about two miles down the shore, on my side of the island. I loaded my guns and moved closer, staying hidden the whole time. I pulled out my perspective-glass, which I had taken on purpose. I laid me down flat on my belly on the ground and began to look for the place. I found there were no less than nine naked savages sitting round a small fire they had made. It wasn't to warm themselves, for the weather was hot. No. The reason was to share some human flesh, which they brought with them.

They had two canoes pulled up on shore. I observed them dancing. I could see their movements but could not tell if they were men or women. The tide started to turn. They boarded their canoes and headed back to the mainland.

I went back to the place where I first saw the bones. I saw that there had been three canoes full of savages at that place. They had left and met up with the other two canoes. This was a dreadful sight to me.

A year and a half passed before I saw any more savages, but I was troubled the whole time.

By now I had been on the island more than twenty-five years. I was surprised once again one morning when five canoes came ashore on my side of the island. Keeping myself hidden, I climbed a hill. Through my perspective glass, I saw thirty men on the beach. They had kindled a fire and were cooking meat and dancing around the flames.

Then I saw two miserable men dragged from the boats. The savages were about to kill them. One of these prisoners was knocked down in the sand. The other, seeing his chance, ran away from them—and he headed straight for where I was hiding!

I was dreadfully frightened. I thought all thirty men would chase him down,

I laid me down flat on my belly and began to look for the place.

and capture me as well. The escaped man ran very swiftly. To my relief, only three men chased after. The runner crossed the creek, swimming with great strength and speed. One of the men following could not swim, and gave up on the shore. The other two swam after the escaped man, but did not swim as fast. As the runner came closer to where I hid, I realized I had the chance to save his life. Then, perhaps, he could help me escape the island.

I ran down the hill. A shortcut took me between him and the men who chased him. I shouted to him. He looked back at me as he ran, and was perhaps as frightened of me as at his pursuers. With my hand, I signaled to him to come back. All the while, I moved closer to his pursuers. One rushed at me, and I knocked him down with the stock of my gun. The other quickly drew a bow and arrow and was about to shoot me. I fired off my gun first, and killed him with a single shot.

The poor savage who had fled now saw both of his enemies fallen. The noise of the gun frightened him, and he stood still. First he looked at his enemies, then he looked at me. He didn't know if I was an enemy as well. I made signs for him to come over. He understood and came a little way, then stopped again. Then he moved a little closer. I signaled for him to come even closer. He came nearer and nearer, kneeling down every ten or twelve steps, to thank me for saving his life.

I smiled at him and he came still nearer. At length he came close to me, and then he kneeled down again, kissed the ground, and laid his head upon the ground. Then, taking me by the foot, set my foot upon his head. This, it seems, was his way of saying he would be my slave forever. I picked him up and put him back on his feet.

We noticed that the savage I knocked down was not killed. He began to

Then, taking me by the foot, set my foot upon his head.

get up. I pointed to him. My new friend spoke some words to me. I could not understand them, but they were good to hear. They were the first sounds of a man's voice that I had heard, besides my own, for more than twenty-five years.

The savage I had saved made a motion that he wanted my sword. It hung from my belt around my waist. I gave it to him. No sooner was it in his hands then he rushed to his enemy and cut off his head with a single swipe. He then buried the enemies where they fell.

Then I took him to my home. I gave him bread and a bunch of raisins to eat, and some water. Then he went to sleep. The other savages must have gone back to where they came from, for no one came looking for the two dead men.

The next day, I gave my new friend some clothes. We noticed that the enemy canoes were gone. I named my companion Friday, after the day of the week in which we met.

—⚶—

Never was there a more faithful, loving, sincere servant than Friday was to me. I made it my business to teach him everything that was proper to make himself useful. Especially, I taught him to speak English. He was a good student, pleased to be able to understand me or make me understand him. Life on the island became so much easier and more pleasant with Friday.

I taught him how the gun worked. I shot a goat and we cooked and ate the meat. After that Friday swore he would never eat human flesh again, which I was glad to hear.

He told me about his nation. He used to be among the people who came to the far side of this island to feast. He was captured in a war and taken here to be eaten,

With our axes, we cut and hewed the outside into the true shape of a boat.

until I saved him. He told me that his home was not far away. It could easily be reached by canoe.

Later he said that among his people lived seventeen white men. "We save the white mans from drown," he told me. They lived in peace among his people, but were near starving. From how he described their wrecked ship, I knew they were Spaniards.

This put thoughts in my head. I believed we could build a boat, sail to Friday's nation and rescue the Spaniards. Then we could take them back to my island where they could live better lives.

Friday and I began to build the boat. I showed him how to use tools, and he was good at it. In about a month's labor we finished it and made it very handsome. With our axes, we cut and hewed the outside into the true shape of a boat. She would have carried twenty men with great ease.

I was gathering supplies to load into the boat when Friday started shouting out at me: "O master! O master! O sorrow! O bad!" He had seen three canoes approaching the island. No doubt they carried more cannibals preparing for a feast.

Sure enough, we counted twenty-one savages and three prisoners. One of the prisoners was a Spaniard, taken from Friday's nation. His hands and feet were tied. The savages built their fire. I gave Friday a gun and we sneaked closer to them. When I gave the signal, we fired. Some of the cannibals were killed. Some were wounded. Some started to run.

While Friday was shooting, I rushed down to the Spaniard and cut the rope that bound him. He was weak with starvation, but I gave him a pistol and a sword. He took them very thankfully, and no sooner had he the weapons in his hands, but as if they had put new vigor into him, he flew upon his murderers like a fury. He killed two right away.

. . . he flew upon his murderers like a fury.

The cannibals that were not killed tried to escape in a canoe. Wanting to catch up with them, I jumped into one of the canoes they left behind. I was surprised to find another poor man inside it, bound hand and foot. He was almost dead with fear. I cut the ropes. He believed that he was being prepared to be killed. I asked Friday to tell him that he was safe now. When Friday saw him, the man and Friday burst out laughing and crying. They kissed and hugged. This man was Friday's father!

We tended to Friday's father and the sick Spaniard until they were well. The Spaniard suggested that he sail back to Friday's nation and bring the rest of the Spaniards here. Perhaps then, all together we could build a ship big enough to sail to the Brazils or the Spanish coast. It was a good plan. We spent six months gathering supplies and getting the island ready for our guests. Then the Spaniard and Friday's father sailed off to get them.

—❦—

Eight days later, I awaited their return. Instead, I saw an English longboat sailing toward the island. It worried me. English ships had no business in these waters. It could only mean one thing: Pirates! Friday and I kept ourselves hidden until we could learn more.

The ship landed and eleven men came out. Three were unarmed and tied up. The three prisoners were left alone while the other men scattered to explore the island. All this while I kept myself hidden in my home. I came out only to spy on what the men were doing. They didn't see me or any sign of my life on the island.

Satisfied that the island was deserted, they prepared to sail off, leaving the three men behind. But by now the tide had turned, leaving the ship aground. I knew it would be ten hours before it could float again.

In the meantime, Friday and I prepared our guns and ammunition for battle. By two o'clock, in the heat of the day, the eight men headed into the woods, I believed, to sleep in the shade. The three men remained on the beach, under a tree. I came as near as I could to them without being seen. Then I quietly called to them. They were startled and frightened, but I soon convinced them that I was there to help.

One of the men was the commander of the ship. "My men have mutinied against me," he said. "Instead of murdering me, they plan to leave me here with my mate and a passenger. They thought this place was uninhabited, and believed we would die here."

I said to him, "If I help you get your ship back, will you take me and my man to England?"

He agreed to. I gave him and his men some muskets. Because the mutineers did not expect us, we were able to capture them.

Twenty-six men were still aboard the ship. They did not know anything was wrong. After a while, when the first men ashore did not return, some more men from the ship came to the island to look for them. We were able to surprise these men as well, and take them under our control. In the battle, the captain who was leading the mutiny was killed.

Some of the men were still faithful to the commander of the ship. When they saw that he was safe and the mutiny was failing, they joined to help him. While Friday and I kept the mutineers on the island under control, the commander and his men boarded the ship and, in no time, took it back.

As soon as the ship was secured, the captain ordered seven guns to be fired. This was the signal to give me notice of his success. I was very glad to hear it,

having watched upon the shore till near two o'clock in the morning.

Having heard the signal, I laid me down to rest. It had been a tiring day. I slept very soundly until I heard the noise of a gun. I awoke to hear the captain call my name. He embraced me in his arms and said, "My dear friend and deliverer, there's your ship!"

There it was! The large ship was ready to carry me away wherever I pleased to go. At first, for some time I was not able to answer him one word, but as he had taken me in his arms, I held fast by him, or I should have fallen to the ground.

The mutineers that lived chose to stay on the island rather than face hanging in England. Before I left, I told them about the sixteen Spaniards who would be coming to the island soon. I left a letter for them, telling them to treat the mutineers fairly.

And thus I left the island, the 19th of December, as I found by the ship's account, in the year 1686. I had been on it eight and twenty years, two months and nineteen days.

In this vessel, after a long voyage, I arrived in England, the 11th of June, in the year 1687, having been thirty and five years absent.

—m—

. . . I held fast by him, or I should have fallen to the ground.